Touchline Terror!

Michael Coleman
Illustrated by Nick Abadzis

ORCHARD BOOKS
96 Leonard Street, London EC2A 4RH
Orchard Books Australia
14 Mars Road, Lane Cove, NSW 2066
First published in Great Britain in 1997
First paperback edition 1998
Text © Michael Coleman 1997
Illustrations © Nick Abadzis 1997
The right of Michael Coleman to be identified as the
Author and Nick Abadzis as the Illustrator of this Work
has been asserted by them in accordance with the
Copyright, Designs and Patents Act, 1988.
A CIP catalogue record for this book is
available from the British Library.
1 86039 021 8 (hbk)
1 86039 592 9 (pbk)
Printed in Great Britain.

Contents

Coach

Left Full
Back

Midfield
(Centre)

Striker

Centre
Back

Goalkeeper

Right Full
Back

Kirsten
Browne

Barry 'Bazza'
Watts

Daisy
Higgins

Colin 'Colly'
Flower

Tarlock
Bhasin

Lennie
Gould
(captain)

Trev the
Rev

Substitute

Midfield
(Centre)

Centre
Back

Substitute

Midfield
(Right)

Striker

Midfield
(Left)

Mick
Ryall

Jonjo
Rix

Lulu
Squibb

Jeremy
Emery

Rhoda
O'Neill

Lionel
Murgatroyd

Ricky
King

1

The Game of the Century

"Get stuck in, Colin!"

"Get back, Colin!"

"Get forward, Colin!"

"Keep going, Colin!"

"Good tackle, Colin!"

"Go on, Colin!"

"Shoot!"

"Goal!! Yes!! Goalie-goalie-GOOAAALLLL!!"

"Well played, Colin! Well played, Angels!"

Colin "Colly" Flower, the Angels FC striker, trotted across to the car that was waiting for him. He slid into the passenger seat.

"Well played, son," croaked the man at the wheel. He sounded as if he'd been shouting a lot.

"Thanks, Dad," said Colly.

"Yep, you played well today. Really well."

The car moved off and Colly tucked his sports bag between his feet. Wait for it, wait for it, he thought. Any minute now.

"Oh, yes," repeated Mr Flower. "Really well."

A gap appeared in the stream of traffic passing along the road outside the park gates. Colly's dad swung the car out and accelerated. Here it comes, thought Colly: "Except for…"

"Except for…"

His heart sank. It was always the same after a match. He would get into the car. His dad would tell him how well he'd played. But then, inside a minute, he'd be saying the two words that made Colly feel as though he wanted to put his head under a heavy blanket. (His own head or his dad's, it didn't much matter which.)

Colly decided to get it over and done with quickly.

"Except for what?" he said.

"Except for," said Colly's dad, "that time you lost the ball in the centre circle."

"Lost the ball? When?"

"In the thirty-eighth minute, it was. I checked my watch. Their midfielder tackled you just as you were turning."

"That was the only tackle I lost all game, Dad!"

"True, true. But it put them on the attack. They could have scored." Mr Flower glanced Colly's way. "That's it, son. Just thought I'd mention it."

Colly waited. "Well…and then there was…" usually came next.

"Well…and then there was that free kick of yours that scraped the bar. I thought you should really have scored there."

"I scored two afterwards, didn't I?" said Colly irritably.

"True, true. Good 'uns they were too. But if you'd banged in that free kick instead of scraping the bar – well, you'd have ended up with a hat trick, wouldn't you? Now, I was watching you closely. You leaned back just a fraction as you hit it. Result – you got your foot under it, see? You need to be over the ball. Get that head down, son."

"Nothing else, then?" asked Colly between gritted teeth.

"Nope. Not a thing."

Colly saw that they'd just turned into their road. That could only mean "Apart from…"

"Apart from…" began Mr Flower.

"What? What? Apart from what?" squawked Colly, his temperature rising.

"That sloppy pass."

"What sloppy pass? I didn't make a sloppy pass from start to finish!"

"Yes, you did."

"When? When?" shouted Colly.

"During the kick-in before the game. When you, Rhoda O'Neill and Lionel Murgatroyd were passing it in a triangle. You went to chip it to Rhoda and hit it too hard and low. She had to run and get it back from that dog. Remember?"

Colly sighed. "I remember."

It was then, as Mr Flower burbled on about relaxing into chipped passes, that Colly came to his decision. He loved having his dad watch him. Rain or shine, hard frost or howling gale, he was always there, the most enthusiastic supporter on the touchline. But these inquests on the way home were driving him bonkers. They had to stop. The question was: how was he going to make it happen?

"Right, everybody, listen in. This is your chance to have your say about a significant world event." Everybody looked towards the man standing at the front of the room.

"What sort of significant world event, Trev?" said Lennie Gould loudly. "Picking the next England team?"

"Striker, Colly Flower!" called Kirsten Browne, the Angels' goalkeeper.

Laughing, Trevor Rowe held up a hand for order. "No, not that. Mind you, if they ever do ask me to leave the Angels and coach the England team, I might well take up your suggestion, Kirsten!"

Everybody smiled. It was rumoured that Trev could have been good enough to play football for England if he hadn't wanted to be a vicar more. Because that's what he was.

The team were all members of the St Jude's Youth Club and Trev, besides being the Angels' coach, was vicar of St Jude's Church. That was one reason why Colly's team were called Angels FC. The other was that Trev insisted on fair play. "Angels on and off the field!" was his motto and the team weren't allowed to forget it. Which made the wicked idea that Colly was about to have all the more surprising…

"No," continued Trev, "the significant world event I'm referring to is the fact that this is St Jude's centenary year – it's 100 years since the church was built. So I'm planning a whole series of special events. And that's where you lot come in. Any ideas for something involving the Angels?"

Everybody fell silent for a moment as they thought.

Then Bazza Watts called out, "How about a football exhibition?"

Daisy Higgins, the team's centreback, wasn't impressed. "What – round footballs, square footballs, oblong footballs, footballs with holes in the middle –"

"You'll have a hole in your middle if you don't watch it," growled Bazza. "I mean an exhibition of things to do with football. We could write to famous people. Get them to donate something. An old football shirt or an old pair of boots…"

"My dad's got an old pair of boots," said Lulu Squibb.

"Has he?"

"Concrete ones." She laughed. "He grows flowers in them."

It must have been the mention of flowers and dads that did it, thought Colly afterwards. Whatever the reason, that's when his devilish idea arrived, whistling into his head like a well-struck shot.

"How about a players versus parents football match!" he yelled.

The moment he heard the suggestion, Trev's eyes lit up. "Colly – that's a brilliant idea!" He began scribbling furiously. "We could call it "The Game of the Century". We could produce a programme. And I'll write officially to the parents, inviting them to put their names forward…"

He stopped and sucked the end of his pen. "Hmm, what about the parents, though? Will enough of them agree to play?"

Colly spoke up straight away. His dad was going to discover that out there in the middle, football was a tough game!

"My dad'll play, Trev. You can put him down top of your list. Number one! Flower, Henry Montgomery. A definite!"

2

Second Thoughts

Colly spent the next couple of days hugging himself with pleasure. What a brilliant idea! It was all he could do to keep quiet about it. He just couldn't wait for Trev's letter to arrive, inviting his dad to play in "The Game of the Century".

And then Wednesday came. During the football season, Wednesday evenings meant Training Over the Park with Dad.

"Let's start with tackling," said Colly's dad. "A good tackle has all your weight going in behind it, son. You lost that one on Saturday because you were off balance. Look, let me show you. I've studied all the best players on the telly, so I know just how to do it."

Mr Flower put the ball on the ground between himself and Colly. "Block tackle, OK?" He demonstrated in slow motion.

"Use the side of your foot and *leeeeean* into it. Right, now try to tackle me."

"You sure?" said Colly.

"Come on, come on. I won't hurt you."

"OK." Colly sighed.

As his dad moved forward to the ball, Colly surged in. Thundering through with his right foot, he hit his dad with one of his best tackles. The effect was dramatic. Mr Flower's right leg was jerked back, his left foot slid to one side – and the rest of him went up into the air.

"Yes...well," said Mr Flower as he picked himself up, "good. You're learning, son. If you'd done that on Saturday, you'd have been all right. Now then. Free kicks."

Again Colly's dad placed the ball on the ground, this time with Colly being sent off to stand between the goalposts. "Point the toe…" Mr Flower demonstrated, looking like a tubby ballet dancer.

Placing the ball on the edge of the penalty area, Colly's dad took five slow paces backwards. Then he ran in, commentating as he went.

"Lean forward. Point toe. Go through the ball. Ooops!"

Colly gazed after the ball as it shot off at a right angle, curving wildly as it flew across the path at the side of the pitch and ploughed into an ornamental pond.

"Did you see how I got that shot to bend in the air?" said Mr Flower as they fished the ball out. "Easy when you know how. Inside of the foot, cutting sharply across the

22

surface of the ball to impart maximum spin."

"I thought you were showing me how to keep the ball down?" said Colly.

"It did stay down, didn't it?"

"Yeh," muttered Colly. "Like a submarine."

As they trudged back to the grass, Colly's heart was sinking like a submarine too. What had he done? Getting his own back by suggesting a parents versus players match had seemed a good idea at the time, but now he wasn't so sure. Come the match, everybody was going to see how useless his dad was at football. And that meant the embarrassment was going to be total.

"Right, son," Mr Flower was saying. "Chipped passes. The secret here is to *reeeelaxxxxxxx*..."

But Colly wasn't listening. He'd just made another decision: Henry Montgomery Flower was definitely not going to play in "The Game of the Century"!

The question this time was: how could Colly stop him?

3

Hitting the Post

Colly lay in bed thinking the problem over. It was tricky. His dad was bound to want to play when he got Trev's invitation. So, was there anything he could say that would persuade Trev not to send one? Not a chance. Colly had been too convincing. So if the invitation was definitely coming, what he had to do was think of some rock-solid reasons why Mr Flower shouldn't accept it once it arrived. Assuming it did arrive, of course.

Colly punched his pillow in delight. That was it! His dad couldn't accept an invitation that never arrived, could he? So, how could he get to that letter first? That would be the tricky bit.

Ever since their nutty dog, Gnawman, had shown itself to be particularly partial to a breakfast of anything that plopped through their letter box, Mr Flower had taken to waiting by the door until the post arrived.

There was only one solution, realised Colly. He was going to have to get up early enough to intercept the invitation before it reached the door. Yes, for the first time in his footballing life he had to make sure he hit the post!

They were into the last minute in the Cup Final. After being 2– 0 down against Manchester United, a brilliant Colly hat trick had put the Angels 3 – 2 ahead. All they had to do was play out time. Winning the ball with another perfectly timed tackle, Colly dribbled it lazily towards the corner flag. Hold on to it, he told himself. There can't be long to go. The crowd are whistling...whistling...

Whistling!

Leaving his dream, Colly shot up in bed. He'd overslept! The postwoman was on the other side of the road, whistling cheerfully as usual. Any minute now she'd be at their door, shoving Trev's invitation into his dad's waiting hands!

Diving out of bed, Colly snatched up his trousers - and threw them down again. No time! If he was going to intercept that letter before it reached their door he was going to have to go just as he was. In his West Ham pyjamas!

Scuttling down the stairs, Colly dived out of the back door and round the side of the house. He was in the nick of time. The postwoman had just reached their front gate as he raced out to meet her.

"Morning, morning," said Colly brightly. "Anything for us?"

The postwoman looked down at Colly's claret and blue pyjamas. "There might be," she said. "Why, what are we expecting? Dressing gown? A pair of fluffy slip-slops?"

29

Colly gave her the sort of glare he usually reserved for defenders who kicked him. "Letters," he growled. "Just letters."

The postwoman handed over a pile of envelopes. Colly quickly sorted through them. There it was! A long brown envelope with a picture of St Jude's Church on the front and their address in Trev's neat handwriting.

Colly shoved it inside his pyjama jacket. Then, keeping it in place by holding an arm across his waist, he padded up the garden path. All he had to do now was put the rest of the post through the letter box and –

"Colin? What are you doing?"

As his dad swung open the front door, Colly stopped dead. This wasn't supposed to happen! His dad must have heard the postwoman go by and wondered why she hadn't left anything. Now what was he going to do?

30

"Er…"

"And why are you in the front garden in your pyjamas?" continued Mr Flower.

Pyjamas! thought Colly. I'm still in my pyjamas! Maybe if I pretend I am sleepwalking…

Slowly, Colly raised his arms and closed his eyes until they were the narrowest of slits. Then he began to totter stiff-legged up the path.

"Post for Mr Flower," he said, talking like a robot. "Post for Mr Flower."

"Colin? Are you all right?"

"Special delivery," said Colin, flicking his eyes open and then closing them again.

Mr Flower frowned. "Overnight delivery by the look of it," he said, staring at Colly's pyjamas. "Are you sleepwalking, son?"

"Yes," said Colly, without stopping. Past his astonished dad he went, up the stairs

and into his bedroom. He'd done it!

Now to destroy that letter. Fishing inside his pyjama jacket, Colly felt for the long brown envelope. It had gone! He ripped open the buttons and looked again. Skin! Nothing but skin! It must have fallen out while I was pretending to sleepwalk, he thought. But in that case, where is it? A sudden shout from downstairs told him exactly where.

"Hey! Colin! Hey!"

Colly flung open his door. There, at the bottom of the stairs, was his dad. And in his hand was Trev's letter.

"There's going to be a parents against players match!" cried Mr Flower. "Trev wants to know if I'll play."

"And will you?" asked Colly.

Mr Flower shook his head slowly. "Oh, Colin. I'm not going to –"

"Not going to?" yelled Colly, his hopes soaring. "Did you say you're not going to play?"

"And upset you, son?" said Mr Flower. "Never! What I was about to say was: I'm not going to miss this for anything!"

4

A Ripping Time

As the days went by, Colly lived in hope that his dad would change his mind. But, if anything, he got more and more enthusiastic about it. Nothing Colly could say would put him off.

"Kirsten reckons the parents team are going to get smashed," said Colly at breakfast two days before the game.

"Oh, yes?" said Mr Flower.

"Pulverised, Lennie Gould reckons," added Colly. "Tarlock reckons you're going to get trounced, Daisy reckons you're going to get dumped, Mick reckons you're in for a mangling, Lulu says it'll be a lashing, Rhoda thinks you're in for a real roasting and both Jeremy and Jonjo think it'll be a joy-ride for us."

"Hmm," said Mr Flower. "How about Bazza Watts?"

"He reckons you're going to get whipped, walloped and whacked," said Colly. "He's bet Lennie that he can kick every parent who's playing."

"Really?" Colly's dad merely smiled. "I think Mrs Watts will have something to say about that. She's playing right wing for us."

"Mrs Watts is playing? You're kidding!"

"No, I'm not. She used to be an international hockey player. And she's not a bad footballer by all accounts. If there's any whipping, walloping and whacking to be done, I bet she'll be the one who's doing it!"

Colly closed his eyes in despair. Not only was his dad going to be shown up by the other dads – he was even going to be shown up by one of the mums as well! Mrs Watts would still be running when his dad was on his knees.

In desperation, Colly had one last idea. If he couldn't stop his dad wanting to play, could he arrange things so that he wouldn't be able to play because he was simply too tired..?

"Dad! I'm worried about you," said Colly, putting on what he hoped was a worried look. "Are you sure you're fit enough for this game?"

"Fit? Me?" said Mr Flower. "Ridiculous question! Of course I am."

Colly grinned. "Then you won't mind coming on a little training run with me, will you?"

"Er…no. When?"

"How about tomorrow evening?"

They set off straight after tea. Colly led the way.

"How far do you want to go?" called Mr Flower.

"Not far," called Colly over his shoulder. "Down to the park, round the boating lake a couple of times, along the towpath by the canal, up to the lock gates and back home through town. Can't be more than ten kilometres. OK?"

"Er…fine," said Mr Flower, already panting for breath. "Fine…"

They got as far as the park – almost. Gasping for breath, Mr Flower collapsed on to the bench just outside the park gates.

"You all right, Dad?" said Colly as he helped his dad home again.

"Course…gasp…I am…gasp…son… gasp," gasped Mr Flower.

"You don't sound it," said Colly as his dad opened the front door. "And you don't look it," he added as Mr Flower immediately flopped down on to the hall carpet.

"Never…judge…by appearances," gasped Mr Flower, his mouth opening and closing like a fish out of water. "A match…is different."

"It is?" said Colly.

"Oh, yes." Mr Flower tapped the side of his head. "You use your head, son. Let the ball do the work…"

"Dad! The game's tomorrow!" Colly shook his head in despair. "You can't still want to play?"

"Of course I do!" said Colly's dad, finding enough energy to sit up. "Why do you think I've bought that lot?" He pointed to a brand-new sports bag, sitting in the corner of the hallway.

"What lot?" asked Colly.

"New football gear, of course! Shirt, shorts, socks – even a new pair of boots. Colin, you won't recognise me when I step on to that pitch!"

This is it, thought Colly. The end. The

absolute end. With brand new gear, his dad was going to look so good that everyone would expect him to play like a wizard. Then they'd learn the truth! Oh, the embarrassment!

As he walked downstairs early the next morning, Colly's spirits couldn't have been lower if the Angels had been bottom of the league with no hope of escaping relegation.

Gloomily he opened the kitchen door, only to be met by Gnawman pounding out to meet him, his tail going round like a windmill.

"Hello, boy. Nice to see you're happy at least."

The dog scampered out to the front door, then back again. Colly ruffled his fur.

"It's Sunday, dimbo. No post today. Nothing to chew…"

As the thought struck him, Colly's eyes settled on Mr Flower's new sports bag sitting on the hall stand.

Could he? Should he? It was a desperate thing he was thinking of, he knew that. But he was desperate. And Gnawman would be forgiven – eventually.

Tiptoeing into the hall, Colly lifted his dad's bag. Gnawman followed him to the front door, panting excitedly.

"Sssh!" Colly said to the dog. "You wait there. You're going to enjoy this."

Opening the front door, Colly stepped outside. He unzipped his dad's sports bag. And then, piece by piece, he began to feed Mr Flower's brand-new football gear back in through the letter box.

His new shirt disappeared in a trice, wrenched from Colly's hand as Gnawman tugged it through. Moments later, Colly heard sounds of ripping.

Colly managed to get one of the new football boots through the letter box next, which Gnawman leapt on as if it were a cat. This was followed by his dad's new socks and finally, his new shorts.

Colly waited for a couple of minutes, then opened the front door. The sight that greeted him was even better than he'd hoped for. Scraps of material were everywhere, with not a thing left that was wearable. In the middle of it all, still chewing happily on the remains of Mr Flower's right boot, sat Gnawman.

Beautiful! With joy in his heart, Colly dashed up to his room to start getting his own football gear together.

Now he really could enjoy "The Game of the Century"!

5

Number One

"You mean your dad's not playing after all, Colly?" said Kirsten, pulling on her goalkeeper's gloves.

Colly shook his head. He tried to look sad. "Afraid not. Bit of an accident in the home, dog-wise."

"That's no good," moaned Bazza Watts. "How am I going to kick my full set of parents now? Your dad should be ashamed of himself."

Not as ashamed as I'd have been of him, thought Colly. He smiled as he remembered what his dad had been doing when he left for the game – holding the tatters of his new gear and muttering to himself about dogs' homes and insurance policies.

"Maybe you can kick him while he's on the touchline, Bazza," laughed Lulu Squibb.

Tarlock Bhasin turned to Colly. "He will be watching as usual, won't he?"

"I reckon so," said Colly as they left the changing room with a clattering of studs. He sighed loudly. "It's such a pity, though. I really wanted my dad to play in this match…"

"I know you did, son," came a familiar voice. "And I wasn't going to let you down. So here I am!"

Colly stopped, open-mouthed. In front of him stood his dad – changed and ready to play!

From behind him he heard loud
spluttering noises, like a collection of
balloons going down. It was the rest of the
Angels team, trying not to laugh.

"Like your gear, Mr Flower!" said Jonjo
Rix.

"Yeh," laughed Rhoda O'Neill. "Where
d'you get it - the museum?"

"No," replied Colly's dad, grinning.
"Out of the attic. It's my old school kit.
When Gnawman chewed up my new stuff it
was all I had left."

Colly blinked. The sight was awful. It was pretty obvious that his dad had grown a lot since leaving school. Everything looked as if it was bursting at the seams. His shirt was tight across his chest and didn't quite reach down as far as his shorts. Or maybe it was his shorts that didn't quite reach his shirt – Colly couldn't tell. Even his dad's socks looked too small, bulging fit to burst with a huge pair of shinpads inside them so that they came only half-way up his legs.

And as for his boots…when Colly saw the cracked and battered things on his dad's feet, with his big toes clearly visible, he wished the centre circle would open up and swallow him whole.

"Hello, Mr Flower. I'm so glad you could play." It was Trev, referee's whistle round his neck.

Colly's dad did a quick sprint on the spot. "All systems go, Trev! Where do you want me? Centre forward, barnstorming through the middle? Out wide, ball-juggling my way down the touchline? What position?"

"What position?" echoed Trev. "In goal, of course."

In *goal*?!

"Well...yes," said Trev. "When Colly said at our meeting to put you down as number one, I naturally assumed you were a goalie. All the other positions are filled now."

"Oh," said Mr Flower. He shrugged. "Oh, well. Goal it is, then. I'll do my best."

In goal! Brilliant! Colly heaved a huge sigh of relief. As he watched his dad trundle across the pitch to stand between the posts, Colly realised that things had worked out after all. OK, so his dad would be hopeless in goal, but that didn't matter. He'd be able to use the excuse that he was playing out of position. And, smiled Colly, with a bit of luck his dad would soon be so muddy that his ancient football kit wouldn't show him up either!

Perfect, he thought as Trev whistled to start the match. Surely nothing could go wrong now.

But it could. And it did. What went wrong was that Mr Flower didn't turn out to be hopeless in goal. Quite the opposite, in fact. He turned out to be sensational. Colly got his first inkling of just how brilliant as Mick Ryall sprinted down the right wing and hit a low cross into the penalty area. Colly hit it on the run. Wallop! Straight towards the bottom corner.

"Goa– " he began to shout…until suddenly Mr Flower flung himself across the goal and tipped the ball round the post!

The applause had hardly died down when Mr Flower did it again. As the corner came over, the ball was nodded out to Colly, lurking on the edge of the area. He met it with one of his best headers, a full-blooded effort which was rocketing towards the top corner - until Mr Flower flung himself up and back to punch it clear.

From then on the match was virtually one-way traffic. Apart from Mrs Watts having a goal disallowed because she was sitting on Bazza as she scrambled the ball over the line, it was all Angels. Only Colly's dad, making one stupendous save after another, stood between them and a famous victory.

"Hey, your dad's good, isn't he?" said Lennie Gould as the whistle blew for half-time with the score still at 0 – 0.

"Yes," said Colly cheerfully. "Isn't he just!"

It was Jeremy Emery who pointed out the drawback. "I do believe that you're not going to score today, Colin!"

Colly frowned. Jeremy could be right - and that would be all wrong too. He didn't mind his dad having a good game, he was delighted in fact, but the last thing he wanted was for him to play so well that he, Colly, didn't score a goal. If that happened his reputation as the Angels' top marksman was going to be seriously dented.

"There you're wrong, Jeremy," Colly said grimly. "He can't keep me out for ever."

But, as the second half wore on, it began to look more and more as if Mr Flower could do just that. Every effort Colly put in was saved. His dad dashed out to dive at his feet when he was put through. He swooped like an eagle to stop his shots. On one occasion he even caught one of Colly's fiercest thunderbolts with one hand!

"Come on, Colly!" yelled Daisy Higgins from the back four. "Call yourself a striker?"

Still 0 – 0 and no more than a couple of

minutes to go, thought Colly. It's got to be now or never.

Suddenly he saw his chance. As his striking partner Jonjo Rix picked the ball up in midfield, the parents' wheezing and spluttering defence opened up.

"Jonjo!"

Colly set off, timing his run perfectly to meet Jonjo's through ball. He looked up. His dad was rushing to meet him, plonking his battered boots down as he ran. Colly didn't hesitate. As his dad got close, Colly feinted to go one way and then darted the other – only to be pulled down by a hand stretching out and whipping his legs from under him.

PEEEEP!

"Penalty!" Trev was pointing to the spot.

"It was an accident, Trev," said Mr Flower. "I went for the ball!"

"Come on, Trev," said Mrs Watts, laughing. "Forgive him his trespasses."

"I have forgiven him," said Trev, trying to look serious. "He should have had a red card. But it's still a penalty."

Lennie Gould, the Angels' penalty-taker, strode forward and carefully placed the ball on the spot. As Mr Flower went back to crouch on his goal line, Colly didn't know what to think. He was happy now. His reputation was intact. If he hadn't been fouled he'd have scored, no doubt about it. So now what he wanted was for the team to win. Or did he? No, he realised, he didn't. What he wanted most of all was for the Flower family to have a double triumph. He wanted his dad to save this penalty and keep a clean sheet!

And he could help it happen! As Lennie paced carefully back, Colly pointed deliberately to the bottom corner of the goal,

to his dad's right. It was where Lennie
always hit his penalties.

Mr Flower nodded. Lennie ran in. He hit
the shot, straight towards the bottom corner
as usual…and Mr Flower dived headlong –
the other way!

A 1 – 0 victory for the Angels! The
players had beaten the parents!

"Well played, Dad," said Colly as his dad drove them home.

"Thanks, son," said Mr Flower.

Colly smiled. Thinking about things in the changing room, he'd decided that, after all, everything really had turned out excellently. He'd played a good game, winning the penalty. The Angels had won the match. And his dad had played a blinder.

Now there was only one thing left to do to make it a perfect day. The final part of his plan swung into action.

"Yep," said Colly, "you played well today, Dad. Really well."

"Thanks again, son."

"Except for…"

Mr Flower frowned. "Except for?"

Colly nodded. He'd taken the bait. "Except for that penalty," he said seriously.

"What about that penalty?" said his dad. "I didn't have a chance. Lennie Gould hit it perfectly."

"You went the wrong way," said Colly. "I pointed to show you which way it was going."

"Ah, but I thought he'd seen you point," said Mr Flower, raising his voice, "so I didn't know whether he'd hit it in his usual spot or change his mind and go for the other side!"

"Good goalkeepers don't watch the ball," shouted Mr Flower, "they watch the kicker so they can work out where he's going to place it!"

"But you didn't work it out, did you?" shouted Colly, even louder.

"Because he wiggled his knees!" bellowed Mr Flower, now going red in the face. "Anyway, what about all the good saves I made!"

"What good saves?" yelled Colly.

"What good saves?" bawled Mr Flower. "What do you mean, what good saves!!"

Bringing the car to a screeching halt, he swung round – only to find Colly grinning from ear to ear.

"Tell you what, Dad. I won't criticise you, if you won't criticise me. Agreed?"

A slow smile spread across Mr Flower's face as he saw the funny side. He put his hand out for Colly to shake. "Agreed!" he said and they both laughed.